INGLISH NONSCENTS

Quick Quips with English

INGLISH NONSCENTS

Quick Quips with English

Michael Nieuwland

Idea Creations Press
www.ideacreationspress.com

IC PRESS   Idea Creations Press
www.ideacreationspress.com

Library of Congress Control Number: 2016961576

ISBN-13: 9780997890419
ISBN-10: 099789041X

Printed in the U.S.A.

FOREWORD

A few years ago I woke up one night with words flying through my head! All kinds of words! They didn't go together, they were not in sentences, they were not tied together in any way. Just words. As I lay thinking about them I realized there must be a reason for this. I got up and started writing them down. The next day I looked at the list still perplexed about it. I put the list away and didn't really think too much about it. Sometime later I got it out and my mind started working. That's how this book got started!

I've always felt that those who come to this country should learn English. That's our language in America and if one is going to live here they ought to speak English. I've come to realize that's easier said than done; but it is do-able!

In 1950 my parents arrived in America; Dutch immigrants looking for a better life. They arrived not knowing a word of English! They had to make their way from Boston to Salt Lake City, Utah on a bus. Not understanding English, at each stop the bus made on that long journey one of them would stay by the bus while the other went to the bathroom or to get something to eat, then they would trade places. They didn't dare leave the bus at the same time not knowing how long the stop would be and afraid of the chance of it leaving without them. They finally arrived at their destination where relatives received them and helped them get started in their new home and a new country. They've told stories of going to the grocery store with a Dutch/English dictionary so they could figure out what they wanted to buy. Stories of catching the wrong bus (they had no car until a couple of years later) or getting off at the wrong place, then having to make their way home somehow. My Dad started school as soon as he could so he could get a good job. I don't have a clue how he managed that! Little by little they learned English. In time they were able to communicate and made a good life here in the states; speaking the language that we speak in America. That's how I know it's do-able!

This book is full of examples of how confusing English can be to those just learning it. Here's an example I noticed in my own mothers English: Take the word "count". Pretty simply right? Now add "-ry" to the end making it "country". If you were learning to speak English you would do what my mother does; pronouncing the word country as "count-ree". Try it yourself: say the word count, then add the -ry still saying the word count. Do it out loud giving it the full effect. It's pretty easy to get confused with! As you will see and read in the following examples, there are words that are spelled the same but have different meanings. There are words spelled differently that sound the same. There are words that have letters that are never heard in the pronunciation. The list goes on and on. As you read these, I hope you will smile and laugh and find the humor I did! I also hope you will quickly recognize the confusion that must come quickly to those trying to learn English. And I wish the very best to those trying to learn! The best way to have fun and find the humor is to read this book with 2 or more people; one reading, the others following with their own copy. In many cases, you have to see the spelling to get the full effect; listening is not enough!

Michael   Nieuwland

I Do certain things. I don't Dew certain things. If I did Dew things, would it mean I sprinkled water on them? That's what Dew is, isn't it? Water or moisture on the grass in the morning? What then is a Hair-dew? Did someone sprinkle water on her hair. How do you do a hair dew? Or should I say "how do you dew a hair dew?

So, I knew a lady that liked to Sew. You say "So what?" or did you say "Sew what?; meaning that you either didn't care that she sews or that you were curious about what she sews. I also know a man that sows. He's a farmer. He sows seeds; meaning he plants seeds. He will later harvest what he sowed. The woman that sews may later wear what she sewed. The farmer will not wear what he sowed; unless he spills it on himself!! This same farmer has a sow. This is not like sowing at all. This is an animal often referred to as a pig. So you need to be careful to listen to what the word sew, sow or sow is referring to. You don't want to think the farmer is sewing in his field nor that the sow is in the house using a sewing machine!

The lady above that likes to sew is called a "seamstress". Some people might call her the "sewer"! Beware you don't make that mistake! A lady that sews is a seamstress; the sewer is the place your toilet flushes into! To call a lady a sewer would create a big stink!

A SOW SEWING

The lady I referred to before that sews sewed a bow. She entered it in the fair and won first place, a blue ribbon. When she went to accept it, the crowd applauded and she took a bow. Well now does that mean she took a bow she had sewed or did she bow to the crowd; meaning she bent forward at the waist showing acceptance of the applause? It could be both. It could be that when she took her bow the bow on her head could be seen. The word bow also has meaning on a ship. The captain said something about the bow. I don't know if that's the front, back, or one of the sides, or if the ship has a bow on it! I don't even know if they pronounce it bow or bow. Which is one of the reasons I don't own a ship! Now I think about it, I was on a ship once. It was a cruise ship. While we were eating dinner one evening there was a man walking around entertaining us with a violin. I happened to notice he was wearing a bow-tie. A violinist plays his instrument by drawing a bow across the strings, creating the sound. He was not using a bow that the woman had sewn; nor did he use the bow of the ship to play his violin. Then when he stopped playing we all applauded and he, like the lady at the fair, took a bow. As I thought about him taking a bow, I thought of when I took a bough. It was a pine bough we used at Christmas. A pine bough is a branch off of a tree, in this case used for decoration. So here we have a bow, bow, bow, bow and bough. Did you say them right as you read them?!! For such a small word, it packs a lot of meaning doesn't it?

When I turned eleven years old, I got a bow and arrows. This had nothing to do with bows, bows or the bow or the bough. It had nothing to do with a ship or a violin. I just got a bow and arrows and since I just thought about it I thought I'd tell you.

Speaking of a ship; I had to ship a package. Oddly the package didn't go on a ship at all. The package I shipped was sent in the mail across the United States where there was no place a ship could go. My package shipped on a truck. If I would have tried to truck my package would it have gone on a ship?

Lots of people get mixed up on when to use "their, they're and there". When they're over there with their car, that's right. If there over their and their looking for there car, that's wrong. Not that they're looking for their car, because it's not there. It's because the wrong words are used at the wrong time. Now, if you're just talking, no one knows how your mind spelled the word you used so it won't matter, just don't try to write it or everyone will be mixed up!

Now this isn't new, but I knew it would come up. If you knew something, it probably isn't new to you. Knew is the past tense of know. That still isn't new to you is it? If only you knew then what you know now .

New is a term of time; if it's new, you knew nothing about it before. If you knew about it before, it's not new now. It's like this: did you know about it? No, I didn't know about it. It was new, that's why I didn't know. If you knew, why didn't you tell me? I don't know; I thought you knew. No, I didn't know and I didn't know that you knew it was new. At least that's settled now.

I went golfing with some friends of mine. There were four of us. We aren't serious golfers, we just go for a good time. It was a busy day and people were backing up at each hole waiting for the group ahead to finish up. Some people aren't very patient though. Especially waiting for four guys who are just having fun! So they got started a little too quick. Suddenly I heard someone yell: "Fore"!! I think it was fore, but it could have been for or four; the sound of his voice didn't give me the spelling. So I learned that if four of you go golfing for a good time and you hear the word "fore", you'd best be watching for golf balls flying toward you, because four and for have already been used so when you hear fore, it means watch out for a ball that was hit too soon that might clobber you!!

Have you heard the term: "I don't have one red cent"? It means I have no money. I was downtown last week and a man approached me for some money. I told him I didn't have one red cent. I hoped he would just leave because he did have a scent! He had more scents than I had cents, but he was asking me for more! It didn't make sense to me. So, I asked him if someone had sent him looking for a cent, he got confused and left me alone; but he also left a scent with me that I didn't want. And he left still without a cent that he had asked me for. He asked for something I didn't have and left me with something I didn't want. He left without what he wanted and left me with something I didn't ask for! Sometimes maybe it pays to have a few cents so you can send someone away that has a few scents. Or maybe keep a few cents because maybe it makes sense. All I really know now is that he was sent for a cent but already had a scent. I was just walking down the sidewalk!

My wife and I have been looking for a house. We saw one we really liked and wanted to know if it had a basement. The owner said no but it had a cellar. I said "Aren't you the seller"? He said yes but there was a cellar underground in the back yard. I asked if that was the previous seller who maybe had passed away. He said I could see the cellar, but I told him I had no interest in that! I just wanted to talk to the seller and he told me again that that was him. I asked how he could be the seller and be talking to me when he said the cellar was underground in the back yard. By now, he told me he didn't think I was the buyer. I said yes I am the buyer, and he said "not on this house"!

We went on vacation a few years ago. We wanted to see the sea. So we went to see the sea. We went to a place where there was a beautiful sandy beach and we saw the sea. It was magnificent! Once we saw the sea we didn't know what else to do. We figured we had seen the sea; which was a beautiful scene, and there was nothing else to see. We came and we saw! Which makes me think of the saw I got. I got a new saw that I saw in the store. I've been looking for a saw and when I finally saw this saw, I knew it was what I wanted. So I bought the saw I saw and I really see why I did. It's really a nice one! You'll have to come see the saw I got and maybe see the sea we saw in our vacation photos. Guess what I'm going to make with my new saw? Of course, a see-saw!!

Have you ever heard the joke: What is black and white and read all over? The answer is: a newspaper. When someone asks that question; because of the black and white reference, peoples minds naturally think of the word read as the color red. So they are thinking three colors. The two words, read and red sound exactly the same. Interestingly, the word read is in itself both present and past tense. Have you read that book or do you think you will read it sometime? The word read also sounds like reed. The president of the company I work for is named Reed. I told him, if you want to have a good read Reed, read the book I read about the red reed. It's a good read.

You know how everyone is dieting these days? Well some people are really impatient when they start dieting. They want these diets to show results almost immediately. They can't wait to start dropping the weight. I guess for some the wait can be almost as bad as the weight. Lots of people want to lose inches off of the waist. But they sit down to eat and put too much food on their plate. Well, they eat it all because despite the waist they want to reduce, they can't bear the thought of the waste. I think they can reduce the waist and the waste by reducing what they prepare and take. I think people need to be patient, wait to drop the weight, wait to see the inches come off the waist and be more careful not to waste.

Some people have trouble with these two words: bin and been. A bin is a type of container that things are put in to hold them. Been is a place you've gone to. Therefore one would say "I have been there" not "I have bin there". If your mother asked you to put these things in that bin you might say "But mom, I have already been to the bin once today". Now in some areas of the country it's common for people to use only the word "bin". "Ya'll bin over to Homers place yet?" "Naw, we ain't bin an we ain't goin over thar". You have to listen carefully because it's another case of not knowing the spelling from the sound of the talk.

Giving someone peace and giving someone a piece is definitely two different things. Let's take "peace of mind". This is a state of satisfaction or of being content. It lets a person be happy. Giving someone a "piece of their mind" is quite unsettling and does not usually bring about "peace of mind". Probably for either party. Usually something has happened that makes one person want to give another a piece of their mind. Whatever happened didn't make the person happy. If they were happy, they would just say something like "That's nice" or "I think that's wonderful". Not being happy, they are going to "give you a piece of their mind"; meaning they are going to tell you how they feel about the situation and you may not like it! So if you want peace of mind, don't stay to listen to someone who's going to give you a piece of their mind. Now, if you are visiting somewhere and they offer you a piece of something, generally you can accept it. "Would you like a piece of cake?" Why yes, thank you. This is a piece of something nice. We all want world peace. This is along the lines of peace of mind but on a larger scale. World peace would bring most of us peace of mind, but if one piece of the world doesn't cooperate, peace is not likely.

This takes us right into "accept" and "except". My wife was asked to donate a cake for the carnival. She accepted the request and already had a whole cake except it had one piece missing. They would not accept her cake. They said it was a nice cake except the one piece missing would make it hard to sell. No one wants a cake with a piece missing! We could accept that explanation (except it was just a small piece!) and baked another cake. To "accept" then is to agree; to "except" is to leave out or exclude.

Change is good. Nothing ever stays the same does it? Change is a fun word! The meaning of change changes with many different definitions. Change is the coins that are in my pocket. Change is what I get back when I give the cashier more money than I owe. To change locations is to move from one place to another. Change your clothes; or a change of clothes. If you take a change of clothes, you can change your clothes later. Make sure you take the change out of your pocket when you change your clothes. My goodness, you have really changed! I need to change my ways. Is that like changing your clothes? How do you change your ways? To change is to move. To move from here to there is to change locations. I sometimes change the change I have from one pocket to the other. It has nothing to do with changing my ways or my clothes. To change your clothes may not mean undressing and putting on different clothes. It could mean the clothes you were planning on wearing aren't right for the occasion and you need to change your choice of clothes. Sometimes when people make up their mind, nothing can persuade them to change.

When I was young, we had a little saying that went like this: "Step on a crack, you'll break your Mothers back". This type of crack was in reference to either a line across the sidewalk or it was an actual crack, where the cement sidewalk had broken. As I grew older "crack" was used in reference to drugs. A "crack-head" was a drug user; or rather a drug abuser. "Crack" is also used to describe a persons mental state. "You're cracked"! means "You're crazy"! I can see where they all fit together. A crack-head really is cracked to be doing drugs and while on them, couldn't care less that he steps on a crack, or better yet, falls into one! And I'm not even getting started on what is referred to as "plumbers crack". Ask your brother!

I like to see the moon at night. Everyone I know likes to see a full moon. It's always so pretty to see that full round sphere in the sky. There are other references to moon that I find interesting. Some men "moon-light". This means they work their jobs for their employers during the day, but at night on their own time, they do work for people usually making some extra money. (normally not reported on taxes I might add!) Then there is the "honey-moon". This is when a couple gets married and goes on a trip somewhere to celebrate together. Then there is what is called "mooning". This is when a person (or the perpetrator) pulls their pants down just enough to expose their buttocks to others! Why they do this I've never really understood. Anyway, I heard about a couple on their honeymoon. They were out in the evening walking under the full moon when a car came by and they were mooned through the window! They, finding this offensive called the police to report the situation. The police came to get a report. When they asked for a description of the car, the couple said that the car was not exactly what caught their attention! They were asked if they could describe the mooners. Well….. Uh…..No. No we can't. I mean, in this sense, one moon looks the same as another, other than maybe the size! All they could say was that under the light of the full moon, they were mooned, but it appeared as two half-moons. Which takes us back to "plumbers crack". Maybe now you understand that one. So, does all of this have any bearing on why newly married couples are called "honey-mooners"?

I like to eat breakfast. It's a rare day that I leave the house without eating breakfast. Lots of days I just eat toast and cold cereal. Sometimes I get on a kick and like a hot breakfast of toast, eggs and ham. Ham is my favorite breakfast meat. Ham comes from pigs. It's interesting that sometimes people refer to another person as a "ham". In an odd kind of way, this is usually a compliment! To call someone a ham is to say that they "act up" in a funny way that makes people laugh. It might be a story or joke they tell. It might be the way they act. Or maybe they act out a story or situation as they tell about it. In any case, to be called a ham is not a different way of saying "you're a pig". Ham is purchased for consumption at the store or at the butcher shop. A "ham" is also something someone does that "cracks" people up. So, one way or another, most people like a ham and some people really eat it up!

Do you get lots of mail like I do? I sometimes feel bad for my mail carrier. Did you notice I said mail "carrier"? Years ago, I never saw anything but mail-<u>men.</u> My mother would ask: "Have you seen the mail-man yet?". Now, it's not uncommon to see a female mail carrier; hence the politically correct term of carrier. Mail that used to be delivered only by a male mail carrier is now delivered by a female mail carrier. So now we have a male mail man and a female mail man but of course she is a female mail woman. Does that mean she delivers femail?

I like toast in the morning. Once my wife made me breakfast and said "Here's your toast". So I of course took it and ate it. Another time, I had done something (I didn't even know what) and my wife said, "You're toast"! Not "Here's your toast", just "You're toast". What was the difference, wasn't it both toast? NO! One was given to me in kindness and out of love. The other suggested that I was in trouble for something I didn't even know I had done. I'm usually quite innocent; like most husbands! Later we straightened things out. We had dinner together and I proposed a toast! Was I asking for toast for dinner? No. Was I asking to be in trouble again? No. This time a toast was celebratory. It was once again a good thing done out of kindness and love, but not to eat. This time we drank our toast.

Look at the word "present".
I got this present for you.
They are going to present the awards tonight.
Will the governor be present at the awards banquet?

So a present is a gift given to someone. It also means to give something. And it is to be somewhere.
So we could say: The governor will be present to present the awards tonight. Since you competed but won't be present for the presentation of the awards, I bought a present for you.

I overheard a conversation between my daughter and a friend. She was talking about a camping trip they had been on. Her friend asked if they have a camping trailer. My daughter answered "No, our camping is in tents". Not really being involved in the conversation, I thought she said the camping trip was "intense". I wondered what had happened that made their trip so intense. When I asked, she told me there was nothing intense about the trip, they just camped in tents. See how easy it is to get mixed up? It was a simple mistake.

Had I had more sense, (not cents or scents!!) I might have been content to stay out of that conversation. Since I wasn't really part of it, I didn't know the content of the conversation. I think a lot of times we could be more content in life not knowing a lot of things. To be content means to be at peace with ourselves. Sometimes the more we know, the more we lose our peace-of-mind and sometimes the more likely we are to give someone a piece of our mind. We already talked about these didn't we? I need to learn to be content with the current content of my writing.

Speaking of "current"! Current events are what's happening <u>now</u>. Right now is the current time. Presently is also now! So speaking of a past experience, but speaking as if I were there again, I could say: "I am currently standing at the edge of the river watching the current go by. I'm glad that I presently have presence of mind to not step into the current as it's much too strong and fast". Current then is the present and at the same time, it's going by quickly! Sometimes the current can be very slow too. This may be shocking to you, but current is also electricity flowing through an electrical conductor. If the switch is turned off, there is currently no current flowing through the wires. Which also means that presently the light is not on. Which by now you might be relating to me; "The lights are on, but nobody is home!!"

While I was standing at the edge of the river, I saw a doe and her fawn. (You know what I mean here right? "A doe, a deer, a female (not femail) deer. Think "The Sound of Music"! OK, now you've got it!!) Anyway, they were beautiful to see! I put my hand in my pocket and realized I had some money there that I had forgotten about. Then it struck me how I was looking at a doe and had some dough in my pocket! I wondered, "Why do we call money "dough"?? Then I realized that there is also dough that we make bread and cookies with. How bizarre! I was glad I was looking at the doe and that I only had dough in my pocket, not dough. That would have been a mess!

Last fall I went hiking with my son-in-law. We hiked a trail that was not steep but did have a lot of rocks. It was a beautiful fall day but we had to watch the trail so we wouldn't fall. Fall is a beautiful time of year but your day can be totally ruined if you fall.

How about someone saying: "you're close to the door, will you please close it?" Hence, the word close obviously has different meanings. If you are close to the door, it designates your location in relationship to the door. If you are asked to close the door it designates an action. So, if you don't want to close the door, don't stand close to the door. Let someone else do it! If there are one or two people between you and the door, it could be a close call.

What is the difference between the following:

That's my watch.

It's my watch.

Keep a watch out!

What is a watch? It is generally thought of as a time piece. It keeps the time of day. Some are battery powered; older models needed to be wound up. They are usually worn around the wrist with a band to hold it in place. So, "That's my watch" simply means someone is indicating that a specific watch is theirs. "It's my watch" may mean that someone is indicating that the watch is theirs. This could start an argument over who's watch it really is! However, this can also mean that they have been assigned to keep watch for a specified period of time and in a specified area. When a person is "on watch" it means they are responsible for looking out for someone or something. They may be looking for animals or people. It may be some "thing" they are looking for. Being on watch may be for the safety and protection of others. So when a person says "it's my watch" they are not referring to a time-piece; they are going to be watching for something. Now to "keep a watch out" is not keeping a time piece out. This would be similar to a person on watch. Or, it could be a mother telling her children to keep a watch out for cars when they are ready to cross the street. Or, if she sees a car coming when her children are about to cross the street, she may call to them: "Watch out!";

again for their safety. So the person on watch needs to be watching for any danger that may come. They may also be watching their watch to see how much longer their watch is before someone comes to take their turn at watch. A good watch is one that will keep time and a good watch will be uneventful. And some people just enjoy watching others. This watching has nothing to do with a time piece, it's just looking at other people to see what they do, how they act etc.

A watch makes me think of hands. You know, the hands of the watch. There's the hour hand, minute hand and second hand. Well, second hand is also when you buy something that someone else has already used. You didn't buy it brand new, it's second hand. Have you ever heard someone say, "Could you use a hand"? Well, most people are fortunate enough to have two hands so I guess that would be a first and a second hand; just like a clock has a second hand. So is an extra hand a third hand? The second hand on a clock is designated because it counts off the seconds in a minute; not because it's the second hand on the clock. I mean, it is but it isn't! What if someone approaches you and says "let me give you a hand"; do they just give you a "hand"?? What would you do with it; put it down and put screws or nuts or nails in it so it could hold them for you?!! And where did they get it anyway? Is it theirs; or did they find it somewhere? Some people are considered very "handy". Does that mean they always have an extra hand available? So you might accept an offer for someone to give you a hand. That person then stays there using their hands to help. So, you might ask them to "hand" you something. This means they use their hand to pick something up and "hand" it or "give" it to you.

Speaking of seconds. Seconds are increments of time. Seconds are also a helping of food after the original helping is gone. Lots of people say: "Just a second", meaning to wait for them a very short time. You might be asked "Would you like seconds"? Is this the same as asking if they need more time? No, this is a second helping of food; unless you need a few seconds to finish what you are doing! They may say, I have to wait a second or they may say "I'm too full, I can't eat seconds".

When you're thinking of seconds, remember that time lost cannot be reclaimed. There are 60 seconds in every minute but there are no seconds on minutes!

To row a boat you need an "oar". At least one, most of the time two. This oar is dipped into the water and given either a forward or backward motion moving the boat forward or backward. You cannot use "ore" to do this. Ore comes out of the ground and is heavy. If you put ore in your boat you are going to add too much weight and there's a chance your boat will sink; regardless of whether you have one oar or two. So be careful to choose; do you need an oar or ore?

My wife and I bought some pears. They were delicious! We told someone else we had pears. They asked us "pairs of what"? We told them we had pears which is a fruit. They asked how many we had and we said maybe 12 or 13. They suggested that we had to have 12, not 13 because 12 would be 6 pairs. Pairs have to be in even numbers. Pears can be any quantity you want. If you tell someone you ate a pear they may ask you what you ate a pair of. Some people will always eat two pears so they don't get mixed up; either way they ate a pear or a pair.

Let's look at the word "address". My address is the designation of where I live. It tells what state I live in, the city within that state and the street within the city. There is also a number that tells which house on the street is mine. In recent years an address has also become the way to reach me on the internet. In the computer world, my address has become the way of knowing where I am and how to contact me. This is called an "email" address. There is another address that has nothing to do with where I live or how to contact me. This is an address given by a person to a group of people. This does not mean someone gave their home address or their email address to a group of people. This means they gave some type of speech. This is also referred to as an "address". "He stood and addressed the people that had come to hear him". Now, if whomever addressed the people wished to give the address of his home or his email address that's his own business. You have to be careful when you address a group of people. You want them to hear your address, but not have it.

I had a friend that had horses. He invited me to come along on a horse ride. I accepted and we went for a ride. My horse wasn't responsive to my commands. He kept doing whatever he wanted. I tried and tried to tell it what I wanted but to no avail. In fact, I went hoarse trying. Odd isn't it? I got hoarse while riding a horse.

I knew a man that loved to sail. To sail generally means to take a trip on a boat. This usually is not a "sail" boat. However, there is a sailboat. This is a boat that is driven across the water by a sail attached to the boat in a manner that allows it to catch the wind and move the boat ahead. So if one hears someone say they are going "sailing" which would they be referring to? I also know a woman (many in fact) who loves a sale. Note that I didn't say "loves to sail", I said, loves a sale. This is to purchase something for much less that it's normal value. Now if the man who loves to sail and the woman who loves a sale are together, they may find a sale on a sail. This could mean they got a bargain on a trip on a boat or it could mean they got a bargain on a new sail for their sailboat. Either way they should both be thrilled. A bargain is a bargain! She found a sale and he gets to sail.

Michael Nieuwland

The above mentioned couple would have to miss out on the sale on a sail if either one of them is in trouble with the law. There is something called "bail". Bail is money used to get a person out of jail; at least temporarily. If her husband was in jail, she might post bail to get him out. Of course, if he were sailing in their sailboat that they bought on sale, he may have needed to bail the boat out. No, the boat was not in jail! If water gets into the boat while you're sailing, you have to bail it out. This is sometimes done with a pail or some other container to scoop water out of a boat. Bailing is not easy! I saw a man who was working to bail the water out of his boat with a pail. By the time he was done he was pale. Not only was he pale from dipping his pail, he was drained! Yes he wanted his boat to be drained, but not himself! This is not to be confused with a "bale". This refers to a bale of goods; a large amount of an item compacted or compressed into a large bundle. You would not want a bale of cotton on your boat with water coming in. It would make it very difficult to bail the water out. All of this takes the fun out of the sail bought on sale. And, you cannot use a bale to get someone out of jail. You need bail. Make sure it's not a pail of water from your sailboat!

The other day I was talking to someone about my foot. I know, that sounds strange! Anyway, it got me thinking about my foot. I realized that my foot is not 12 inches long, but 12 inches is also a foot. So my question to you is: is your foot a foot?   If your foot isn't 12 inches long is it still a foot? A foot then is part of your body that you stand on; but also a measurement of length; 12 inches; 12 inches also being known as a foot. Now, if I have to buy a pair of boots; I want them to fit my feet. I buy a pair because I have two feet; one boot for each foot. Notice the difference of pronunciation? Why do we say boot different than foot? They both have two vowels; "oo" between two consonants. Try saying foot like you do boot or the other way around!! You might get tongue tied!

Have you ever tried replacing a pane of glass? My Dad tried it once and it was a real pain! My siblings and I had broken the pane and while my Dad was attempting the replacement we were doing something that made him upset. In trying to discipline us he accidentally put his fist through the glass pane which in turn really caused him some pain. The pane was glass, the pain to replace it was an anguishing experience because of having to do it and the pain was a literal physical hurt caused by breaking the pane. The pain of replacing the pane was intensified by the pain it caused.

I have a son that is quite bright; meaning that he is very smart or intelligent. The sun in the sky is also quite bright! You should never look directly at the sun, it will hurt your eyes. You'll see spots for hours afterward, if not something worse! I can look directly at my son and it doesn't bother me at all. It may bother him more than me! My son who is quite bright knows better than to look at the sun which is quite bright. Thus, the word bright means a degree of intelligence but also means a degree of light. The sun is very bright; the moon and stars not so bright. My son is very bright, but there are other people not so bright. They are the ones confused by all of this!

Do you know that a rabbit is sometimes also known as a hare? Have you ever touched a rabbit's fur? Sometimes it's soft like some peoples hair. So both a hare and hair can be soft to touch. Some magicians use rabbits in their shows. They pull a rabbit out of a hat that appeared to be empty. They use rabbits because if they said hare, people might become confused whether the magician was pulling a hare out of a hat or if his hair was being pulled out. Sometimes people say they are going to pull their hair out; often when they are frustrated about something. They are not magicians! Have you ever heard of a "bad hair" day? For a magician that could be a "bad hare" day. If the rabbit, or hare, didn't come out of the hat when expected, it could be a bad hare day; prompting the magician to want to pull his hair out when pulling a hare out is what caused his frustration in the first place!

Here are some things that sound odd but have been said:
"I'm blind you see".
"My sense of smell stinks".
"His fingers were cut off and he didn't feel a thing".
"That he can't walk is a lame excuse"
"I can't smell that stinker".
"I dig using this shovel".
"The power in electricity is shocking".

Which of the following doesn't fit:
Look, Book, Boot.
Answer: Boot; it's the wrong size!!

Here are some deep thought questions:

Does a horse ever get hoarse?

Do bees break out in hives?

Do nylons really run?

Does toothpaste ever get a brush off?

Do we knead bread?

This got me thinking; can three people communicate with each other when one is deaf, one blind and one dumb (meaning they can't talk)? The Blind would not see the deaf person use sign language or read their lips. The deaf would not hear the blind speak but could read signing if the dumb person could sign. The dumb could hear both the deaf and blind speak, but often deaf people don't speak either. So the deaf could read the lips or see the signing of the blind and dumb, the blind could hopefully hear the deaf speak and the dumb could hear the blind speak and hopefully the deaf if they can talk. They may have to help each other communicate by telling one or another to tell the third party. This is not making fun of people with handicaps, it's just a thought that came to me. If you think anything about this, don't be angry with me; think about how blessed you are if you are not handicapped with these situations.

This also reminds me of some other things I've heard people say, "I can't hear you, it's too dark"! Someone else said, "It's so loud I can't see anything"!

Have you ever wondered about words like: Gnat, Knight, Knife, Psychiatrist, Psychology? Why do we have to have that first letter on these words? Sometimes I have to spell a word; especially on the phone. You know how the letters B, P, & T (and others!) are easy to mix up? So you say a word that starts with the letter you need that makes it very clear which one you're using, right? Next time you need to use a "P", tell the person: "the letter "P" as in "psychology"!! Or if you have to use a "G", tell them "G; as in Gnat"! In many cases this will confuse the person more than help them, but it's a lot of fun and you're likely to get a chuckle out of them! Try saying those words by pronouncing the first letter which is normally silent. Go ahead, **G**nat, **K**nife, **K**night. They sound silly don't they? But guess who got away with actually using a company name doing the same thing: K-Mart & T-Mobile are two!! I wonder how some other corporations would do with a similar spelling? Psams Club? Kwalmart? Pshopko? Gtarget?

While we're on spelling, how about these two words that sound the same but are spelled entirely different: "busy" & "dizzy"! I think we need to change busy to bizzy. When I see the word busy, I think it has something to do with buses. So if the road has lots of traffic, we call it busy. But if there are a lot of buses, we should call it "busy". It's very bizzy here with all the buses. When I see so many of them moving around and it's so bizzy, it makes me dizzy! (so said my daughter Lizzy!)

Look at the spelling of the following words; then listen as you say the words:

Guy; tie; my; sigh; eye; sky. Now to me these words need to be re-spelled like this: guy should be "Gi". Tie should be "Ti". My should be "Mi". Sigh should be "Si". Eye should be "I"; but that conflicts with "I", meaning me or myself. Sky should be "ski"; but then it would be confused with ski which when you have a pair you can slide down a snowy slope; so ski has to become "ske" (not skee)!   Here are some examples: I hurt mi I when that Gi saw mi ti. This gi caught mi I and I just had to si. I tried to ti mi boot. Mi ske came off and flew through the ski. I was afraid it would hit the gi I saw with mi I which made me si. Oh mi this is confusing! Why do we spell so many different ways when the pronunciation is the same!?

Here are 4 words; all spelled different but sound the same:

When I was <u>eight</u>, I was <u>late</u>, but so hungry I <u>ate</u> the <u>bait</u>.

Why not all the same:

When I was ate, I was late, but so hungry I ate the bate?

Or: when I was eight, I was leight, but so hungry I eight the beight?

And there's that "gh" again that I don't hear; why are they there?

Some more spelling & pronunciation issues:
Home & some; spelled the same, the only difference is the consonant at the beginning of the word. Now, say "some" like you same "home". Why do they sound different? The way we say "some" sounds the same as "sum". We take some numbers, add them together and come up with the sum, or total. Did you notice the word "come"? Spelled like "some" and "home" but sounds like "some". If you say come like you say home you have a "comb" to use for your hair. And why is there a "b" at the end of comb? If there is a bee on the end of my comb, I'm going to throw both the comb and the bee away from me! Either way, I don't see the necessity of a "b" or a bee on a comb.
Now add these words: hum, from, thumb & numb. Even though "from" is spelled differently, the way we pronounce it, it still sounds like hum, thumb & numb. But here again, you have a bee on the end of each word. Now, if the bee on the end of your thumb stings, your thumb may go numb. That's OK because you won't feel it anyway! Aren't you glad there isn't a B on "bum"?! Again, why don't we spell sum or hum with a "b"? Here are more words with the letter "b"on the end: limb, tomb & bomb. Again, two of these words are spelled the same with the only difference being the first consonant. Did you notice the pronunciation? Why don't we pronounce these two words the same way? If you say bomb like tomb you have boom. It now becomes the

sound the bomb makes when it explodes. If you are near the bomb when it explodes there is a good chance you might lose a limb or end up in a tomb. A limb is an arm or a leg on a person, but also a branch on a tree. Often bees live in trees so to have a bee on the end of a limb is not so unusual! Bee's can be a real problem, but why do they have to cause so many problems on the end of words? Maybe it's time we let this be.

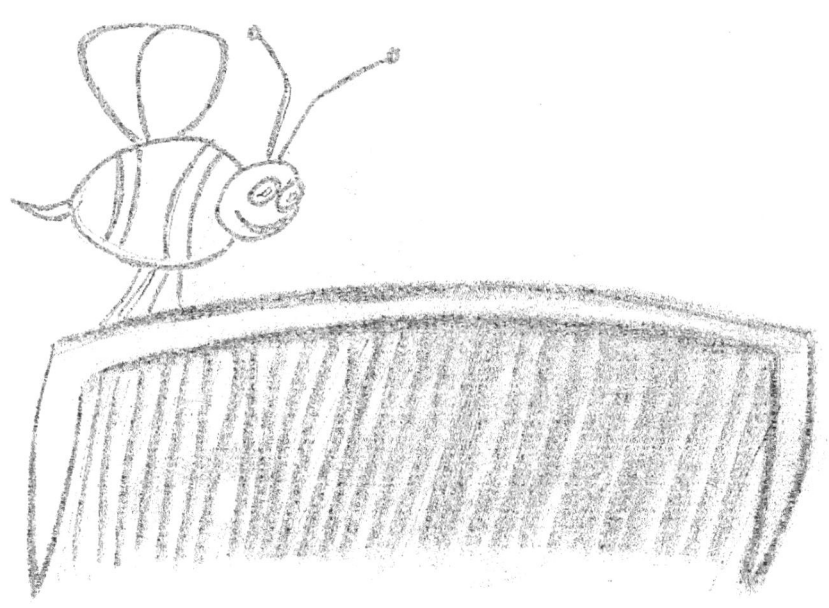

Let's look at the word: charge. A "charge" card is used to pay for something. The person using the charge card will later have to pay the charges. Charge is also the word used when an individual or group moves forward with intent or motivation to accomplish something. This "something" is oft times an opposing group or individual. In some cases, like a good Christmas sale, a crowd will "charge" a store and "charge" their purchases. If the crowd is in a frenzy, and emotions are out of control, the charge of the store could be dangerous and people could (and do) get hurt. Someone might be "charged" with battery. Did they purchase a battery on their charge card? No. If someone "charges" someone else, (or attacks someone) they are in danger of being accused of and charged with "battery". This person has not been purchased on a charge card! The term battery in this case means "assault". If a person attacks another person with batteries, they could be charged with battery with a battery. But, a battery is also needed for the operation of some toys or equipment. The toy needs to be charged with a battery. Or it needs a charge from a battery. In this case, the battery is a unit that holds or stores electrical power to operate something. So a battery with a charge is a good thing. But being charged with battery is not good. Being charged from a battery is necessary. A battery cannot charge with a charge card, but it can give an item a charge to make it operate. Some batteries can be re-charged and some cannot. This doesn't mean they are purchased again, it means when they have lost their power, they are recharged, which is to say they have a fresh store of electrical power in them. Someone has to be in charge of these batteries. To be in charge is to oversee or supervise people or things. The person in charge needs to make sure that the batteries charged are charged. They also need to make sure there is no battery taking place. Batteries charged, should always be charged or someone will be very unhappy!

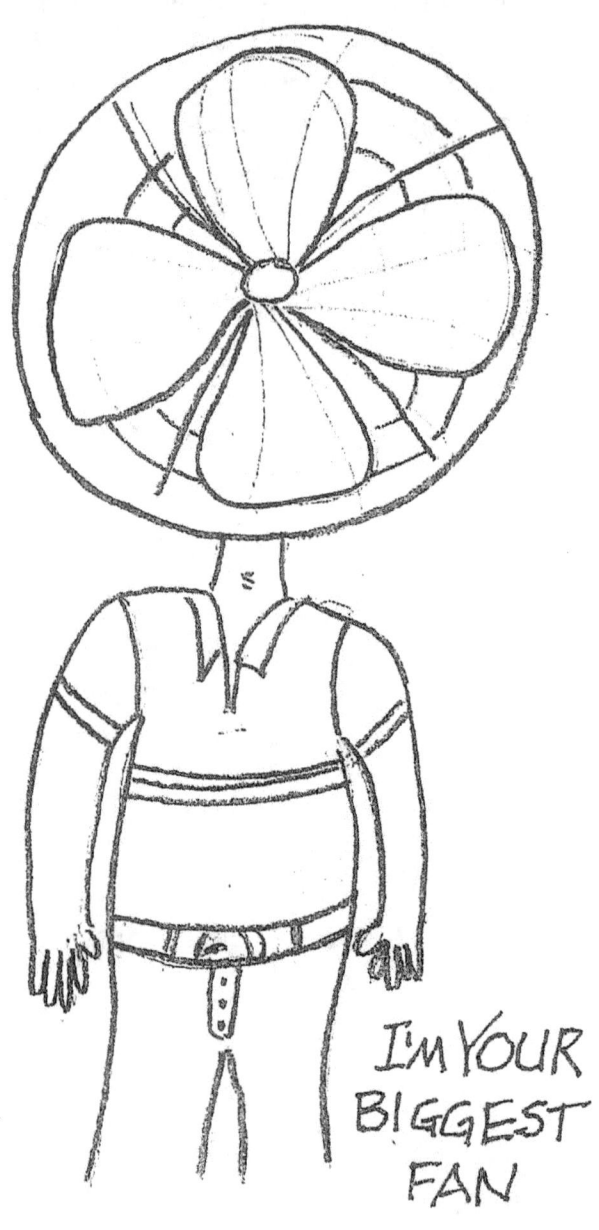

I'M YOUR
BIGGEST
FAN

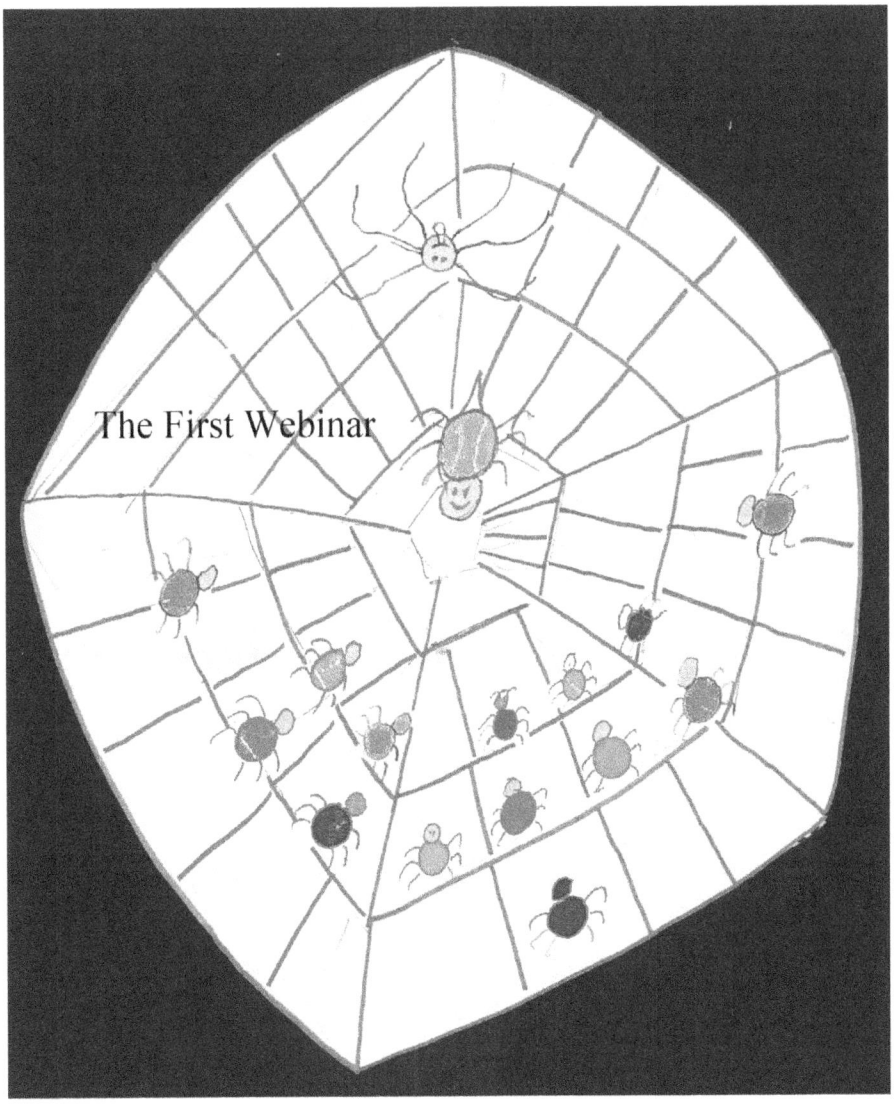

RUNNING NOSE

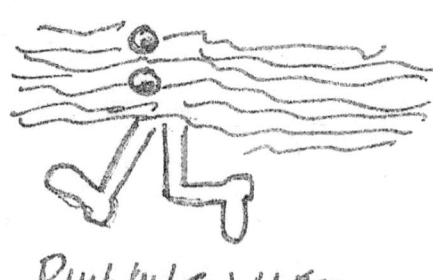

RUNNING WATER

NYLONS RUNNING

TOW TRUCK.
TOWING A TOE

TOE TRUCK

Michael Nieuwland

Here's a brain teaser! Corn is grown on stalks. There are kernels of corn on an ear of corn. When the corn is harvested there might be quite a stock of corn. This is not the stalk it was grown on. The stalk is the plant that grew out of the ground, stock is the amount of corn available for market. So are ears of corn anything like your ears? I hope not! Ears of corn have long green leaves around them. Inside these leaves and coming out of the top are strands called silk. To pull all of this off of the corn is called "shucking" the corn. I have never seen anyone (and hope never to see anyone) with ears that look like ears of corn! Now, there is also a military officer title called a "Colonel". Believe it or not, this is pronounced "kernel"! Isn't that corny!? Sometimes corn gets stuck between your teeth, especially if it's corn on the cob. Can you imagine a Colonel eating corn and getting it stuck in his teeth? Someone might have to tell him: "Colonel, you have a kernel stuck in your teeth!". In the military, to tell a Colonel something like that, Generally one would take him aside and tell him Privately! Any other way could be a Major mistake! And can you imagine someone making a mistake in making a name sign for the Colonel? It would say "Kernel Potter"! He would become the laughing stalk (or stock) of the military! I can imagine the sign makers response: "Shucks, I didn't know"!

PLAYING THE
PIANO BY
EAR

Speaking of vegetables, do you know how many carrots it takes to make a diamond? The answer is "none"! When I was young, I heard diamonds referred to as "X" number of carrots. I never understood what carrots had to do with diamonds. Well, I finally came to realize that my spelling was wrong. The worth of diamonds is measured in "Karats", not carrots! I still don't know just what a Karat is, but at least I no longer wonder about the relationship of carrots and diamonds!

I've never known a man by the name of "Herb". But I've heard the name before. I've also heard of plants people grow and use as medicines or seasonings called "herbs". However, despite the same spelling, these plants are not pronounced with the "H" but without it; like "erb". So how does this work? I believe that Herb the gardener invented these plants. They became Herbs Herbs. People got confused! So they got a little lazy and just started saying "Herbserbs". Then of course, other people started growing these Herbs and so Herbs was dropped and erbs became the name. In honor of Herb, the spelling was kept the same. It's a little like the chicken and the egg, did Herb come first or did Herbs come first?!

Lets look at the words tire and retire. A tire is commonly known as the round inflatable rubber piece that is mounted on a car or bicycle wheel. This is the part that actually touches the road surface. Add a "d" to tire and you have "tired". Does this mean the tire has been mounted to the wheel so it has been "tired"? No, this means that I have been doing something that has taken all my strength and now instead of being energetic, I am tired. I need a rest! Logically then, to be retired means that I got tired once and now I'm tired again, so I am retired. Or, it could mean that the car got new tires once and now it's getting new tires again, so it has been retired. The commonly known definition of "retired" is a person whom has worked for a period of time and has reached either an age or a level of success that allows them to "retire"; meaning they no longer have to work. "No longer work" is relative however, since many people who retire feel that they work harder now that they're not working. That means that working can be better or worse than working depending on the work. So, if you need a tire for your car, go where people are working with tires. Just for fun ask if they will "retire" your car! If you tell them you are retired but working hard, it may encourage them to keep working. Does this work for you? I got tired writing it; re-read it and got tired again. I wasn't "re-tired"!

BEAR ARMS

BEAR NAKED

BEAR FOOT

BARE FOOT

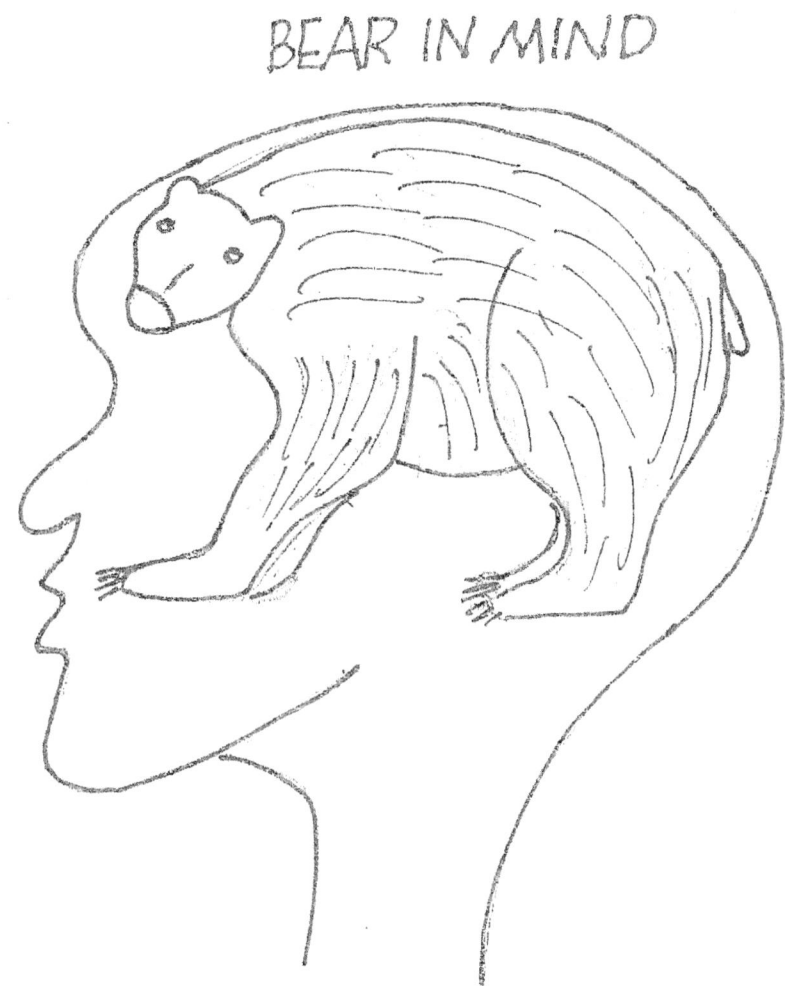

BEAR IN MIND

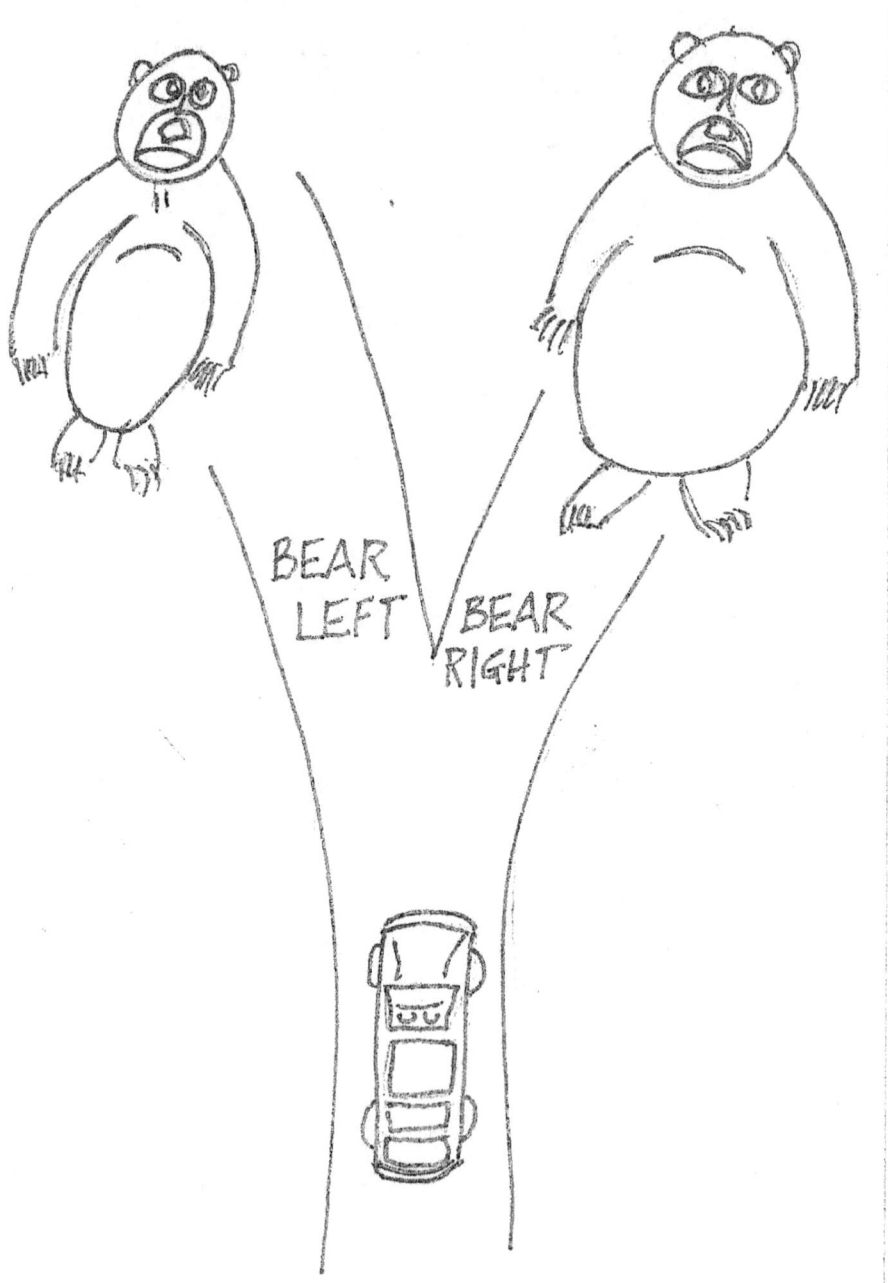

BEAR WITH ME

I got up early one day and sat just letting my mind wander. I realized I was feeling blue. I noticed the sky outside was blue and I noticed that the wind blew. I found it odd that I was awed that the sky was such a deep blue. It was early and I was going to bake bread. I wanted to get busy before it got too hot. I knew that to bake bread you need to knead the dough so it will rise. I wanted my bread to rise before I saw the sun rise. I didn't knead the sun so it would rise. I heard the phone ring and it reminded me to take the ring off my finger before I needed to knead the dough. When I took off my ring it made me think of the 3-ring circus we had recently seen. What a scene lay before us as we entered that circus! As I headed for the kitchen to start my bread, I tripped over a shoe and had to shew a fly away because I didn't want it in my bread. I got started but my mind was still wandering. I thought about the principal at our elementary school trying to teach a principle. The children were to draw something. Most kids will draw their family, in stick figure forms. One child wanted to draw a gun! One child drew a bear. The teacher told him to draw fur on it, but the child said it was bare; a bare bear! The principals principle was that guns and bare animals were not appropriate in school. When he spoke some kids raised their hands and said "we can't hear over here". We realized that just when the principal spoke, a boy rode by the window with a baseball card hitting his bicycle spokes! The drawings the kids were doing were for a contest. I never did hear which one won! I did hear about one child who drew a whale and when he heard he didn't win, he began to wail. He thought he should have drawn a herd of whales instead of just one. Then he may have won. The wail that kid let out was a noise that really annoys me! Later when the kids went out for recess, they played ball. Several children wanted to take the ball out. The teacher chose a number between 1 & 15 and the one who guessed the right number won. Once they started playing they all had a ball! On show and tell day, two boys brought bats. One bat was used for playing ball. The other bat was kept in a jar. His dad had caught this bat one night when it was out flying around. For a science report one child chose rocks. He had three catagories of rock; rock a baby to sleep, a rock band and a rock he had picked up off the ground. After all these thoughts went through my mind I decided I better get on with my bread making. I realized the sky was still blue, but a lighter blue. The wind still blew, but I wasn't so blue. These thoughts had made me smile! I knew I had to reign in my thoughts and suddenly wondered if it would rain today. I also knew I had to concentrate on what I wanted to accomplish. To help me, I got a container of concentrate out of the freezer and made orange juice. Then I got started on my bread.

One day while working in my yard I picked up a stick which had blown out of a nearby tree. It occurred to me that the meaning of "stick" could quickly and easily be changed by simply adding "-up" to it. It was now a "stick-up"! A simple stick had become a very serious thing! To "pick up a stick" was no big deal. To be involved in a "stick-up" was something entirely different.

Here are some other words you can change the meaning of just by adding a letter:

Take the word "but". "But" means to take exception as in "I would go with you *but* I am busy". Add another "T" and you have "butt"; pronounced the same as "but". This could be a cigarette butt, to butt heads (to oppose each other), to put two pieces together end-to-end. Now one more, add an "e" to butt and you have "butte". This is a steep hill with a flat top. This time the pronunciation is changed as well as the definition.

Try the word "slim". This describes a slender shape. Add an "e" to slim and you now have "slime". With the help of only one letter we went from something generally pleasing to see, to something considered disgusting!

Look at the word "tin"; a thin metal. Add a "Y" and you have "tiny"; something very very small. One letter can make all the difference!

Now try adding a letter to the word: "say". Add the letter "s", making it "says". Now pronounce says the same way you pronounce say! Have you ever heard anyone say says like that? The way we normally say says, sounds more like "sez"! When you read this did you say says, or sez?!

Look what you can do with just one word; the word "head". Move ahead. Get ahead. Head it up. Head them off. Over your head. Trail head. Head ache. My head hurts. He's a bone-head. I have a head cold. You're a hot head. Head of the class. Heads up! Forge ahead. Head of lettuce. Head out. Head in!

Use your own head to come up with more!

A Boy standing on his head.

Jumping into water over your head.

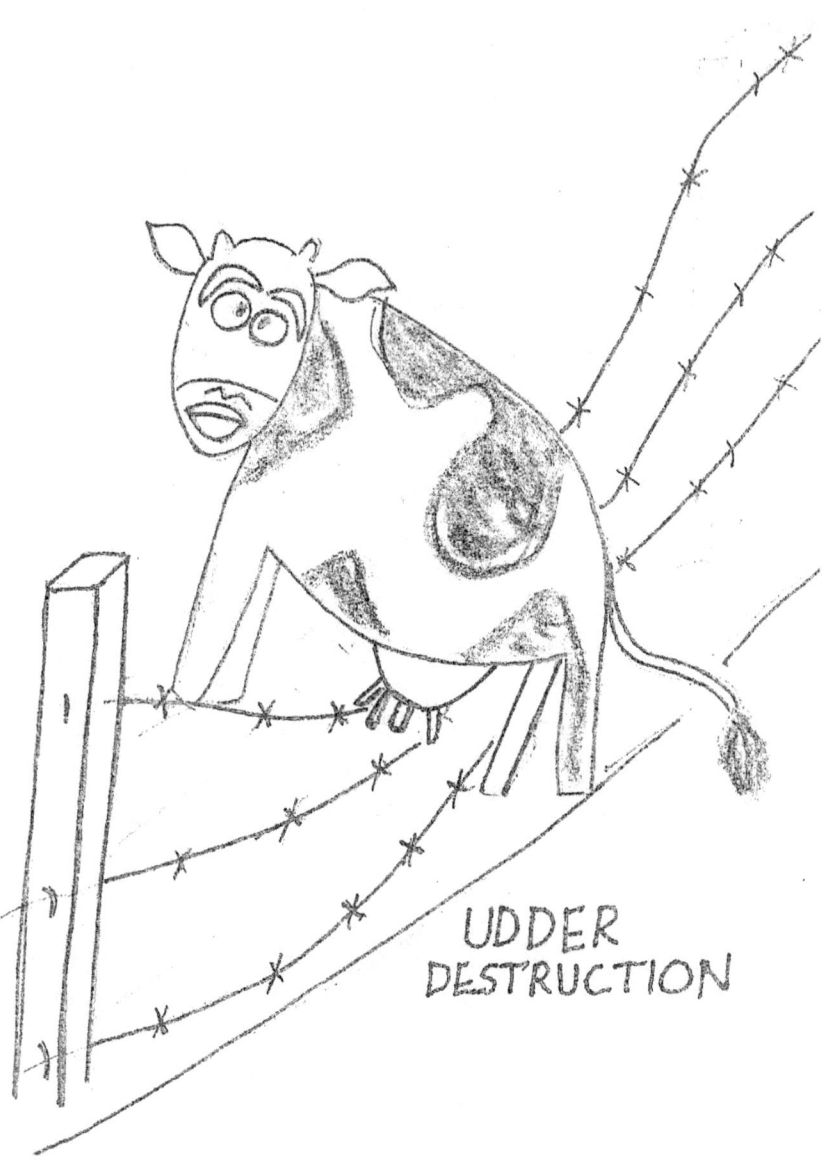

UDDER
DESTRUCTION

Do you know what a "ewe" is? Did you ever see a ewe? It's nothing to be sheepish about! A "ewe" is a female sheep. Now you know!

Did you know that cows have udders? The udder is like a bag hanging from the bottom side of the cow toward the rear legs. The udder holds the cows milk. This is not to be mixed up with "utter", though when we pronounce these words they often sound the same. To utter is to make a noise or to speak. Utter also means complete or total. So if a cow tries to cross a fence and it's udder gets caught, the cow is likely to utter, or make a noise! If the cow isn't helped, it may mean utter destruction of the udder; or in other words, udder destruction!

That story makes me shudder. Shudder is not to be confused with "shutter". A shutter is usually found on a house, these days mostly for decoration. Shutters used to be used to protect windows. The shutters, made of wood would be closed and latched over the windows in a storm to protect them. If the storm was really raging, the people inside might shudder from cold or fear; which means to shake or tremble.

If you look in a dictionary at "de-"; one definition is "to reverse the action". I wondered how that works with some words. To de-grease would mean to take something that got greasy and take the grease back off of it. So lets look at the word "deceased". This refers to someone or something that is dead. Then look at "ceased" which we know as "having stopped or ended" So logically speaking, to "decease" would mean to reverse what has ended which would mean bringing back to life! So why do we use a word that means life to describe someone as dead?!!

What became of all those kids you knew in school?

My old flame became a firefighter.
That drip became a plumber.
I was shocked to find out he's an electrician.
One started at the ground level and became a landscaper.
He wanted to branch out so he went out on a limb to prune trees.
He is a roofer; he's always been on top of things.
Someone else became a roofer but got a bad case of shingles.
That stud became a carpenter.
He thinks he's cool installing air conditioners.
She really blossomed when she became a florist.
Her becoming a florist stems from her love of flowers.
I see he became an eye doctor.
He got his foot in the door and became a Podiatrist.
He wanted to work in the glass industry but his hopes were shattered.
She is heavily into weight loss.
She's a chef, she always has something cooking.
He started his hunting business with only a buck.
That liar is now a politician.
The kid that was always horsing around owns a dude ranch.
A boy no-one thought would ever straighten up is a Chiropractor.
A girl that always got hammered on the weekends does nails.
He was a druggie in school; now he's a pharmacist.

Here's news in the sports world:

Lots of people are getting a kick out of Karate.

New studies show that most basketball players dribble all the time.

Basketball is considered a foul game by some.

Baseball players have been out on strike three times.

Some baseball players are out standing in their field.

When baseball players are traveling they often have to make a short stop.

Most baseball fields have more bats than originally thought.

Tennis players are most considerate of each other; they're constantly serving.

Selling souvenirs at the tennis games has become a real racket.

There was stick up at the hockey game. The ref called a penalty, others called the police.

I think it's pretty slick how they clean up the ice arena.

The problem at the equestrian park is a lot of people just go horse around.

There are several golf clubs you can join.

A lot of golfers like to putter around on the greens.

Some golf courses have EMT's on staff because of a increased number of strokes experienced on the course. Many feel that an increased number of strokes is the cause of an increased number of strokes.

Look at the words "patience" and "patients".
A doctor has a number of patients. He must also have patience. Sometimes he may have lots of patients & lots of patience. He may need a lot of patience with his patients. A hospital needs patients to operate; without patients there would be no need to operate. A surgeon will operate on a patient in the hospital. Either way, patients are needed for both doctors & hospitals to operate. Parents often need patience with their children. This does not mean they have to go to the Dr. office or the hospital to get patients. A patient is a person in a Doctors or hospital care. Patience is to calmly endure something; often something difficult.
Now, back to "operation". If a hospital didn't have patients, no-one would be there and they could not operate. The operation of a building is to keep it's systems working properly; heating and air-conditioning; lights, plumbing. Keeping it clean, keeping doors, windows, toilets, sinks etc. working. How does the building operate? Very well, they have a well trained staff to keep it operating so efficiently. How do doctors fit into that? They don't work on furnaces, A/C units, sinks, etc. They operate on patients (mostly in hospitals). These patients have problems that require an operation, often referred to as surgery. This means that Doctors also need patients. Without them, operations would not be necessary by the Dr. or in the hospital!
Hopefully you are patient, but not a patient. Hopefully you

won't have to be a patient with a doctor that has no patience. If you are, he will have at least one patient, but perhaps still no patience. And finally, I congratulate you on having the patience to read this!

Speaking of hospitals, I've heard that most surgeons are pretty serious people. I guess in order to instill confidence in their patients, they have to be serious and not cut up too much!

Getting back to the hospital; here are some real explanations of doctors:

Oncologist; the doctor on call

Cardiologist: A card shark

Intern: holds everything in; needs psychiatric help

Proctologist: a study in the solar system and the planets. Especially Uranus.

I had a number of problems with math. I'm not sure how to sum it up but I think I just wasn't equal to the task. It just didn't add up to me no matter how many times I tried. The problems just seemed to multiply. I only understood a fraction of what the teacher said. When others tried to help me I tried to reciprocate by helping them. Sometimes I just couldn't find a common denominator. Then I heard someone say "squared". I thought they were talking about me? When we talked about Pie I finally thought I understood, but it wasn't the pie I thought it was.

At one time I was very interested in a mine. The kind of mine that might have monetary value. So I bought a mine. Mine was a mine that I had to mine. Some thought it just looked like a worthless hole in the ground. But I was proud of this mine of mine. I began to mine my mine. It was hard work. Those who saw it only as a hole in the ground began to change their minds after I started to mine my mine and found valuable things inside! Sometimes you can't just see a hole, you have see it as a whole. The hole is often just the beginning and doesn't show the whole picture.

The word "Light" has some interesting meanings. Sometimes it refers to the weight of an item. Sometimes it refers to how bright an area is. Sometimes it's used in reference to a "light fixture". One might say, "This package is very light"; or "It's not very light in this room"; or "Turn on the light". The switch to turn on that fixture is the "light switch". Not because it's light weight but because it is associated with and connected to the fixture that produces the light. Or it could sound something like this: "I turned on the light with the light switch so I could find that light package". Light can also be referred to as a thought coming to ones mind; or receiving understanding. When that happens the person usually says something like: "Ah, now I understand"; or "Oh, the light just went on"!

Did you know.... The record shows a record number of records were recorded!

I needed a loan at the bank so I went to talk to them. I went alone because I knew I could qualify for a loan alone. I got the loan. Now I alone have a loan to pay back.

It's funny what people find out about themselves; sometimes in the oddest of ways and at the least expected moments. I ran into an old friend one day that I hadn't seen in years. I was surprised that I recognized him, but moreso that he recognized me. I mentioned that to him and he said he recognized my nose! Of all things, my nose! I never thought I had a prominent nose. This guy said he knows my nose. Now after reading this I bet you'll be a little self conscious wondering if someone knows your nose! (and after looking at this doesn't "nose" seem like a funny little word?!)

You've seen a fly, right? An insect that flies around and is generally pretty obnoxious. We swat them with hands, fly-swatters, newspapers etc. Well, I have a fly on my pants. Be careful if you're thinking of swatting this fly! I may not want you to! This fly doesn't fly; it zips or buttons! Often we want to kill a fly, but other times a fly is necessary. Now if there is a fly on my pants but no-where near my fly; go ahead and swat; I don't want or need two flies. The button or zip fly allows us to loosen our pants for ease of pulling them on or off. This insect that flies is just a pest. Now an airplane can also fly. When we are in an airplane we say we too are flying. A fly in an airplane can still fly. It can fly while it is flying! We can only sit in an airplane. It's just a form of speech when we say we are flying. There are other ways someone can fly. If I am running and trip, I might fly through the air. If I'm in a fight and get thrown through the air, I am also flying. So I guess it has to do with being "airborne". So why is a fly called a fly when other flying insects have other names? I guess the fly got there first and had first choice of names! How about a butterfly? Should it really be called a "betterfly"? After all, it's a lot "better" than a regular fly! Besides that, butter doesn't fly! What about a "gnat"? Why isn't it a fly? Gnats are really obnoxious. They even got a name with a letter they don't even need!

Have you heard the terms "work-it-in" and work-it-out? When do you use "in" and when do you use "out"? Well, if you have a problem, you have to work-it-out. If you have something to do but already have a full schedule, you have to work-it-in. So I had a problem and had to see the doctor to work-it-out. When I arrived the nurse asked if I had an appointment. I said I did not but told them "I have a problem; I need to work-it-out with the doctor". I asked if they could work-it-in on their schedule. I knew if I was patient they could work-it-in and I could work-it-out! After all, I really was the patient!

Here are three words; spelled different but sound the same:
When the dog took a <u>bite</u>; my butt went <u>tight</u>; and I stood
straight up to my full <u>height</u>.

Have you ever seen something so odd you couldn't stop
looking? I saw something I thought was so odd, I was awed.
In fact, you may have been awed seeing how awed I was at
how odd this thing was.

Here are some examples of words with a "gh" in them:
through, fight, tight, ought, sought, bought, caught, thought, though, taught.
When you say these words, do you hear the letters "gh"? I don't! Let's examine these a little closer.
I am through with this; I am threw with this. But the word threw has a different meaning; I threw the ball.
I closed my fist tight and punched him which started the fight. All this when we just went to fly a kite. Why didn't I close my fist tite and start the fite? Or why didn't I skip all that and just fly my kight?
Though I thought I might get caught, I still bought the item I sought.
(I still don't hear the "gh" in any of this!)
Maybe we should change all this to the following:
Tho I thawt I mite get cot, I still bot the thing I sot. Doing it this way, you might get caught on the cot. And this one will really throw you off: neighbor. I don't hear the "eigh"at all. I hear: Naybur. I went to see my naybur when he came home. There's also the number eight. At my birthday party when I turned ate, I ate my birthday cake.
Then there are these words with a "gh" that sound like "f": rough, enough. Who ever said we get the sound of an "f" out of a "gh"? They sound like they should be spelled "ruf" and "enuf".

How about these: I don't know why but I was so shy I gave a big sigh before starting to cry because I couldn't buy anything at the fish fry. Why, shy, cry & fry; at least they look the same. Why are sigh and buy different but sound the same? Shouldn't they be "si" and "bi"?

Right, left and wrong. This seems like a strange combination of words. Let me show you how they are related:

I was driving down the road when my passenger told me to turn left. Here's how the conversation went:

Turn left.

Right (I should have said OK here!)

No, left!

I know, I said right.

I don't want you to turn right, you need to turn left!

I didn't say I was turning right, I was acknowledging you!

So, I turned left but it turned out it was wrong. I made a left turn that should have been a right turn, so it was really a wrong turn. So right and wrong can also be correct or incorrect. Right and left also determine a direction. You have to be careful when driving and giving directions. Whenever you turn left you could be right or wrong. If you turn right, you may still have gone left, (I made a left turn but it was right) or again, you might be wrong. I hate turning anymore because right or left, I'm afraid it will be wrong!

If you just got into this and don't understand, you may feel left out. If you do, you're wrong, and if you think about it you'll know I'm right! There is nothing wrong about feeling left out and you know that's right.

You didn't know I could write about right, left & wrong did you? That's OK, you're not the only one left that didn't know and that's all right.

Do you have a pair of glasses? Do you wear glasses?
Many people wear "eye-glasses". They are used to correct vision that is not clear. People that can't see well, use eye-glasses. But normally they are referred to simply as glasses. We also have drinking glasses. These are containers made of glass that hold liquid. We put the edge of the glass to our lips and when the liquid leaves the glass it enters our mouth so we can drink. Can a person wear a pair of these glasses over their eyes to correct their vision? NO! Glasses and glasses do not interchange with each other and perform the others function! Drinking glasses are likely to distort ones vision more than it was before; and eye-glasses will not hold liquid for drinking purposes! My wife asked if I had seen her glasses. I brought her two glasses from the kitchen cabinet, but she said she couldn't use them! I was at a family gathering when someone asked who's glasses these were. They were cleaning up after dinner and there were two drinking glasses. I told them they weren't mine; I was wearing my glasses!

A PAIR
OF EYEGLASSES

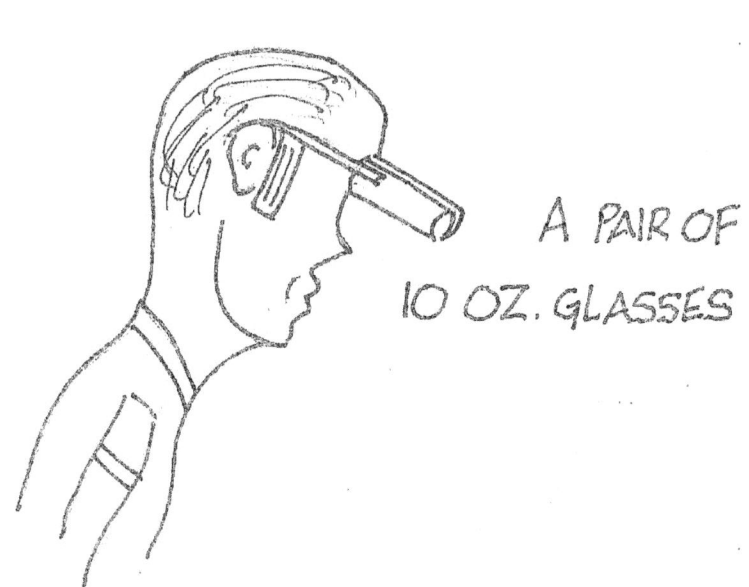

A PAIR OF
10 OZ. GLASSES

Do you know what a "board" is?
Have you heard of "board & room"?
Is there a "Board of Education" in your area?
Do you know kids who are "bored *with* education"?
Have you ever had to "board" an airplane, train, or boat?

A board is a flat piece of wood. With this understanding, board & room means: if you rent a room, you get a board with it. And why would you want a board with your room? Does Board of Education mean that everything you need to learn is on a flat piece of wood? What is the difference between Board of Education and Bored with Education? What has all of this got to do with when you board a plane, train or boat?

Board, a flat piece of wood. Some one is going to use this board to make something. Maybe it will be part of a house, a cabinet or furniture.

Board & Room. This is when some one rents a room; but included in what they pay to rent the room is "board". This means they are also provided with meals.

Board of Education is a group of people; or administrators whose responsibility it is to regulate the affairs of, or make decisions regarding policies of a number of schools under their direction.

A "Board" can also be a council who will decide whether a person may be qualified for admission to an academic program etc.

Bored with Education is what happens to a lot of students who have attended school for a long period of time. They may not be challenged, or they may have lost interest. Maybe they simply don't feel or see the need for further education. It is often the responsibility of the Board of Education to decided what to do with those who have become Bored with Education!

To Board a plane, train or boat is to get on with the intent of traveling on the said mode of transportation.

So let's put this all together:

One of the hobbies of a member of the Board of Education is woodworking. He works with a board to make something. Sometimes he cannot work with this board because he has to attend the Board of Education meeting. He leaves one board to go to another. Fortunately he pays board & room so he has a place to live and his meals are provided. At the Board of Education meeting they discuss what to do with those who have become bored with education. He is told that there is a conference on this subject that the Board of Education wants him to attend. It is in another state, he will have to board a plane to get there, then board a train to complete the trip. When he returns he will again work with the board he is using for his woodworking project and he will again work with the Board of Education to resolve the problem with those who are bored with education. While he was gone, he realized that the Airplane boarded several other board members who are attended the same conference he did. Many of them seemed bored. He also noticed that there was a train transporting thousands of boards across the country. These boards were intended for use in building something.

Here's a simple word: roll. Kids can roll a ball across the floor while their mother eats a sweet roll for breakfast. While this is happening, they tell the dog to roll over. I've heard that if you're being attacked by an animal you should roll over and play dead! At school the teacher has a role with the names of the students in class. The teacher may also have a roll on the desk to eat. A student might explain to another that that is the teachers roll, or that the teachers role is on the desk. Teachers may also be role models for kids in their classes. This may help some kids realize what their role is in class or in life. What role do you play? Do you like rolls?

A GIRL WITH MOOSE IN HER HAIR

Do you mind? Do you mind? Do these mean the same thing or something different? The answer is yes! If I am in line and need to reach across another person I might say: Excuse me, do you mind if I reach over? Another time I might ask a child who is misbehaving: Do you mind?; meaning do they listen and obey when they are told something? If I start a sentence and then stop halfway through, I might say: "never mind, I changed my mind". Watch other people when you do that; they may think you've lost your mind. I hope you don't mind me writing about this; it can be a mind teaser.

Have you ever seen a moose? Have you ever seen deer? Have you ever seen my dear daughter put mousse in her hair? Oh dear, it's a sight to see!

Here are some fun words to play with:
Bore; That woman bore five children.
Bore; I hate to listen to him; he's such a bore.
Bore; To drill a hole.
Boar; Be careful; I just saw a wild boar.
Bored; He drilled some holes.
Bored; To be totally uninterested.
Board; We already talked about this one!
Sore; I have a sore on my leg where I got scratched
Sore; It's really sore; it hurts!
Soared; The airplane soared overhead.
Sword; His sword was very long and sharp.

Do you know how to use the word "Shot"? I looked at a piece of equipment I had that had been left outside. It was rusty and the parts wouldn't move anymore. I said, This thing is shot; meaning it was damaged and no longer usable.

I bought a gun recently and went to the shooting range. I shot the gun several times to see if I liked it. I know a man that got very angry because he had a gun that didn't work. He tried shooting the gun but couldn't. Finally he got a another gun and shot the first one!

Some people go to bars where drinks are served. There is a very small glass called a "shot" glass. No, it's not for small people! And it hasn't been shot by a gun! It's just a small drinking glass.

I went to the doctors office because I didn't feel good. He said I had the flu and sent the nurse in to give me a shot. She did not come in to shoot me with a gun! She did not give me a drink in a shot glass. She gave me a shot in the arm with a syringe; sometimes called an injection. After the shot I got, I almost would rather have been shot!

Then I went to work and made a mistake. The guys I work with really made fun of me. They took some "pot shots" at me; meaning they made some remarks about what I had done that were kind of joking, but had some serious tones in them. Pot shots are always done at someones expense. (No, a pot shot does not mean someone shot a pot with a gun!) I knew a guy that took a shot but missed because of the mist.

But it was hard to tell if he really missed because he couldn't see if he missed through the mist.

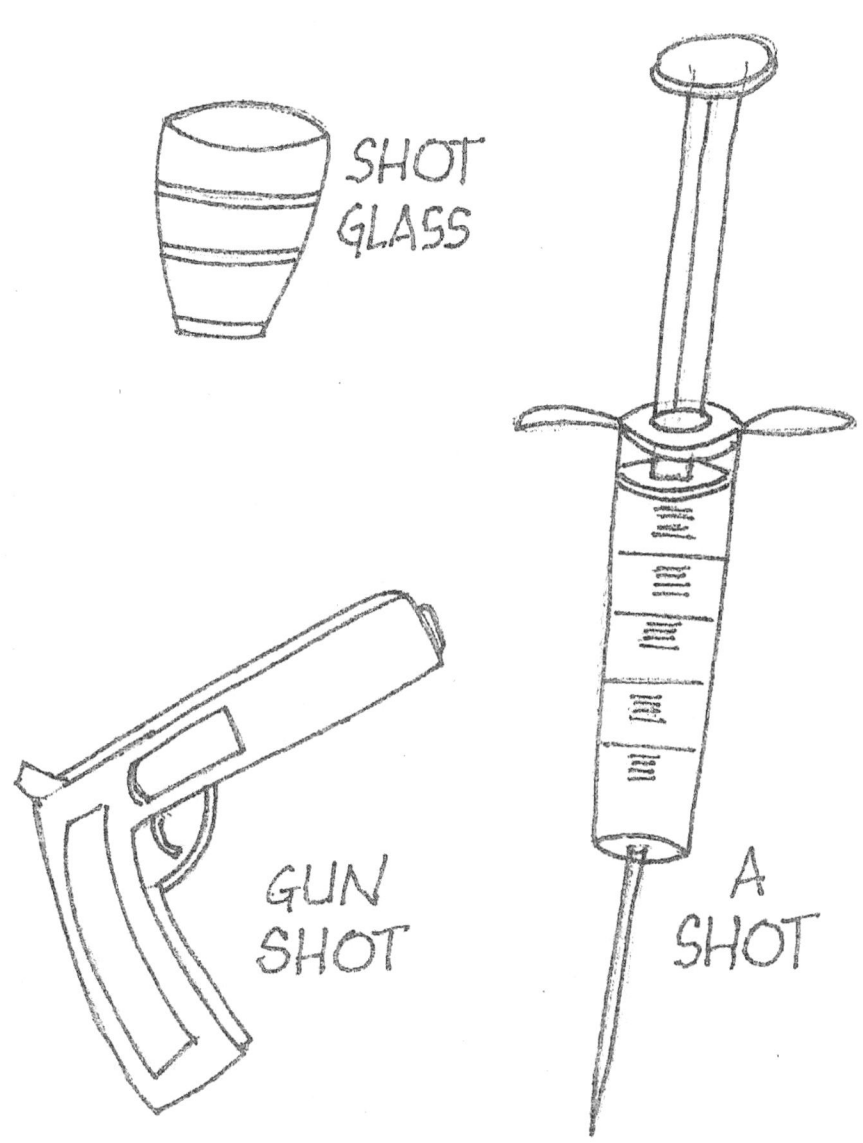

SHOT GLASS

GUN SHOT

A SHOT

Here's a word you can have some fun with: Gas. Gas is a liquid we put in our cars & trucks to make them operate. Without gas, they won't run. Some gas is called propane gas; which we use for our BBQ grills and camp trailers. Gas is also what we use to operate furnaces and some other appliances. It is piped into houses and other buildings. It is in a vapor form. It is often referred to as natural gas. There is another natural gas. Guess where it comes from?!! People, and some animals! This type of natural gas can make people and animals really uncomfortable and can be absolutely painful. It can even make other people who don't even have gas uncomfortable! Most gases have an odor. You can smell the odor of gas you put in the car. You can smell propane gas. You can smell natural gas. They all have their own distinct odor. Sometimes you can smell the other natural gas that comes from people or animals. It doesn't always have the same odor! Sometimes it's hardly detectable and other times you notice it and just want to leave, or run! The other gases I mentioned are purchased for our use; we have to pay for them. This last natural gas doesn't cost anything; in the sense we don't have to pay any money for it. This gas is built up in the body; usually as a result of something eaten. The gas for cars, BBQ's, appliances, trailers will ignite if exposed to flame; like a match. This can be very dangerous; it can cause an explosion and fire. One should never attempt to ignite the natural gas that comes from humans or animals! Someone is going to get burned and it's not going to ignite anyway! Never attempt this!! Gas for cars is dispensed from a hose on a gas pump. Gas for a BBQ type tank is dispensed from a large tank into smaller ones through a hose and with pressure. Human and animals dispense gas naturally; it's called "passing" gas and is also often times under pressure! It usually comes from their back-side; hind end or bum; depending on the terminology used! Most of the time, this happens by surprise and is rarely controllable! It is often accompanied by an explosive sound, a hissing sound, or like an air leak; similar to holding the neck of a balloon and letting the air escape! Sometimes it is silent; no sound at all.

What does the word "wind" make you think of? Did you think of the wind that blows leaves off of the trees? Did you think about that old watch you had to wind so it would keep time? When you read the word, did you say wind or wind? When you had to wind that old watch, did you say you winded your watch? No, you wound your watch. Wound is the past tense of wind. But yesterday when the wind was blowing did you say it winded? No, the wind blew! Now some people get excited or sometimes frustrated with a situation and they get wound up! If they get too wound up they might be winded by the time they're done. If they get too wound up they could get hurt and get a wound. Let's try a story line with this:

I had to wind my watch as I listened to the wind blow. The wind blowing got me wound up; while I wound my watch. I couldn't get around much because of the wound I had. I get really wound up about that wound. I got my wound when I was running down a windy road on a windy day. I ran so far I got winded. I didn't wind my watch, but I whined when I saw it wasn't working anymore. It was my fault, I didn't whined my watch.

I'm sure that you use a bowl at your house. A cereal bowl. A mixing bowl. Every house has another bowl; a toilet bowl. Both being called a bowl; are they the same thing? Maybe you use a bowl in the kitchen to mix a cake batter. When the batter is done you pour it into a cake pan. You scrape out the batter with a spatula to empty the bowl. Remember earlier how we talked about how one letter can make a huge difference? With one letter you can turn a bowl into a bowel. A bowel also needs to be emptied regularly. No scraping is necessary or recommended! This is where the toilet bowl comes in! The bowel is emptied into the toilet bowl which also needs to be emptied. This is much easier than scraping the mixing bowl; you just push a lever. Easier than a self-cleaning oven! Now don't get mixed up; you don't want to keep any bowels in your kitchen cabinets! And you don't want to empty a bowel into a bowl used for mixing cake batter. Each one has it's place and purpose. (Once when helping my sister-in-law move we noticed a box carried into the house marked: "Bowels". No one knew whether it went in the kitchen or the bathroom and no-one dared open the box!) How does "bowling" fit into this?

Let's go back to the batter mixed in the bowl. There is another kind of batter. This is a person holding onto a bat waiting to hit a ball thrown toward him or her. This bat is a long wood or aluminum piece used to hit the ball in a game called baseball. It is not the type of bat that flies through the air! The person holding the bat waiting to hit the ball is called the batter. The person making a cake with the batter in the bowl is probably called a baker. Whatever you call them they are not holding a bowl with a batter standing in it waiting to hit the ball. The person who throws the ball to the batter is called the pitcher. The pitcher throws the ball to the batter so he can hit the ball with the bat. However, the pitcher hopes that the batter will NOT hit the ball! You may be thinking: If the pitcher does not want the batter to hit the ball, why don't they just hold the ball instead of throwing it to the batter? It's a contest to see if the batter can hit the ball or if the pitcher can throw the ball in a way that the batter, even if he tries, cannot hit the ball. When the pitcher takes a rest from pitching the ball he may need a drink. Some people serve drinks out of a pitcher. This is not pouring liquid out of the baseball pitcher, a pitcher in this sense is a container, usually with a handle which holds a drinkable liquid. The liquid is then poured into smaller containers for drinking out of. So the pitcher throws the ball to a batter, and the pitcher is used to quench the thirst of the person mixing the batter.

One day I was sitting in my bathroom, kind of waiting for something to happen! (I'm sure you can all relate to that!) I looked at the scale on the floor and it had the word "Health" on it. I realized that it consists of the word "heal" and they added a "th" to make health. There is also the word Heel. A man hurt his heel and had to wait for it to heal. Now, if you say health but pronounce it like heal with a th, it will sound quite odd! Try it: say health but pronounce it like heal plus the th.. If we're going to keep saying health like we are used to, it should be spelled: Hellth.

Now when you talk to me don't talk so loud. I'm right here and I can hear you! Yes I heard you last time, you mentioned something about that herd of cows you heard about. Why are heard and herd two different spellings? You and I both heard cows, but I do not herd cows, only you herd cows. If you herd cows, you probably heard them the whole time you were herding them.

Tear, do you mean tear or tear? I tear up at a sad story. My eyes get wet and the tears run down my cheeks. I tear up my paper when I make a mistake. You tore up your paper? Can you say: I tore up after the sad story? No, but you can say: I'm all torn up about that sad story. Do you remember how many tiers were on that wedding cake? Were people crying over the wedding cake?

No, tiers are levels. The cake had 4 levels or tiers on it. Four cakes stacked on top of each other. When I heard they weren't getting married, I was quite torn up about it and the tears fell freely. If the tiers of the cake fall freely the cake will be ruined and make a mess!

Have you ever seen the Super Bowl? This is the biggest football game of the year! Are there other bowls; just regular size ones? I think there's a restaurant (or there should be!) that offers different sizes of soup bowls. They also offer a Souper Bowl! It's the biggest bowl they have! You can get this all year; the Super Bowl is only once a year.

There was a hole in the wall at my house. I finally decided to fix it. I had to fill in the whole hole or there still would have been a hole. A smaller hole but still a hole. If you don't want a hole you have to fill in the whole hole; not just part of it. I filled in the whole hole and patched it up. Now you can't tell there was ever a hole.

Getting tired of telling students what to do the teacher said: I am only going to tell you this one more time; I've already told you two times and that's two too many to have to tell you. I agree with her too.

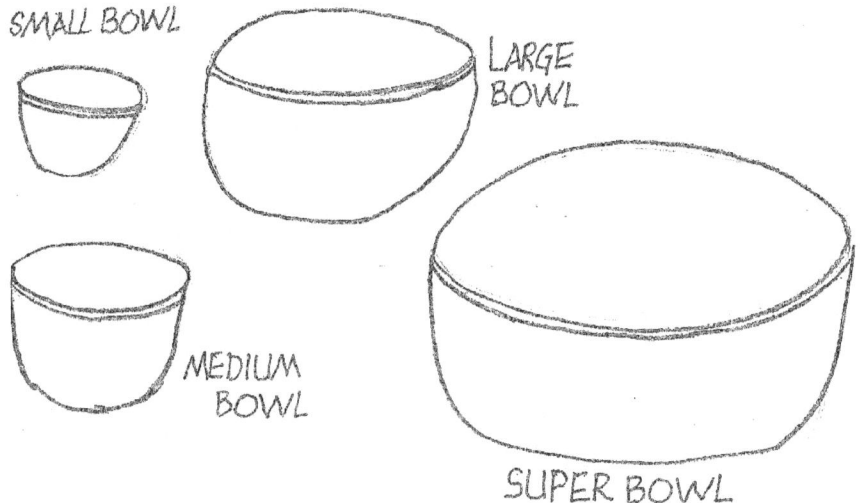

SMALL BOWL

LARGE
BOWL

MEDIUM
BOWL

SUPER BOWL

Michael Nieuwland

Michael Nieuwland

Michael Nieuwland has never written a book. He had so much fun writing this one he decided it was time to share it with the world. His hopes are to help people smile and chuckle a little and for a few minutes leave the stress and worries of daily life behind. He has earned no degrees but has received the 3rd degree multiple times. He has received no awards but did win first place in the Pinewood Derby during his 8 years in Cub Scouts. He still proudly displays the winning Pinewood Derby car and trophy in his home office! He was given a commemorative watch for 10 years of service at his job when he completed his 16th year of service and after 35 1/2 years of total service there has never seen any other such jesture of appreciation. Based on the content of his writing, his wife Frances requested that her name not be specifically mentioned. Michael and his wife reside in Taylorsville Utah.

InglishNonscents@gmail.com

Michael Nieuwland